I ♥ U

Little Mamá

Forgets

Robin Cruise
Pictures by
Stacey Dressen-McQueen

Melanie Kroupa Books
Farrar, Straus and Giroux
New York

In memory of Jessie and Robert Cruise—and for their grandchildren
and great-grandchildren —R.C.

With love to Ron and Finn, and for Emma Nelson
and Gertrude Dressen with love and happy thoughts —S.D.M.

Text copyright © 2006 by Roberta A. Cruise
Illustrations copyright © 2006 by Stacey Dressen-McQueen
All rights reserved
Distributed in Canada by Douglas & McIntyre Ltd.
Color separations by Chroma Graphics PTE Ltd.
Printed and bound in the United States of America by Berryville Graphics
Designed by Barbara Grzeslo
1 3 5 7 9 10 8 6 4 2

www.fsgkidsbooks.com

Library of Congress Cataloging-in-Publication Data
Cruise, Robin, date.
Little Mamá forgets / Robin Cruise ; pictures by Stacey
Dressen-McQueen.— 1st ed.
   p. cm.
Summary: Although her Mexican-American grandmother now forgets
many things, Lucy finds that she still remembers the things that are
important to the two of them. Includes glossary of Spanish words used.
ISBN-13: 978-0-374-34613-3
ISBN-10: 0-374-34613-5
[1. Grandmothers—Fiction. 2. Memory—Fiction. 3. Old age—
Fiction. 4. Family life—California—Fiction. 5. Mexican Americans—
Fiction. 6. California—Fiction.] I. Dressen-McQueen, Stacey, ill.
II. Title.

PZ7.C88828Li 2006
[E]—dc22

2004040462

Spanish Words and Phrases

a la derecha (ah lah deh-REH-chah)	to the right
a la izquierda (ah lah eez-KYEHR-dah)	to the left
bonita abuelita (boh-NEE-tah a-bweh-LEE-tah)	pretty grandma
buenas noches (BWEH-nahs NOH-chehs)	good night
buenos días (BWEH-nohs DEE-ahs)	good day (or good morning)
cielito lindo (see-eh-LEE-toh LIN-doh)	beautiful sky (from a traditional song)
delicioso (deh-lee-see-OH-soh)	delicious
Duérmete mi niña . . . (DWEHR-meh-teh mee NEE-nyah)	Sleep, my little girl . . .
Luciana María Isabela Gálvez-Molinero (Lu-see-AH-nah Mah-REE-ah EE-sah-BEH-lah GAL-vehz-Moh-lee-NEH-roh)	Lucy's grandmother's name
mamá (mah-MAH)	mama (mother)
mi pequeñita (mee peh-keh-NYEE-tah)	my little one (for a girl)
sí (see)	yes
¡Te amo! (teh AH-moh)	I love you!
Tembabichi (Tehm-bah-BEE-chee)	a fishing village in Mexico

*L*uciana María Isabela Gálvez-Molinero.
My grandmother's name is a quiet morning song.
But some days, Little Mamá forgets . . .
to wake up with the sun.

I tiptoe into her room.
Then, as softly as her shadow,
I tickle her awake!
"*Buenos días*, my little Luciana!" Little Mamá says,
stretching like Paco, my cat.

"Wake up, lazybones!" I say,
stretching like Little Mamá and Paco.
Even when she forgets I'm BIG, not little—
and my name is LUCY, *not* Luciana, like hers—
my little *mamá* remembers . . .

to tickle me right back!

Some mornings, Little Mamá forgets . . .
the bread she is toasting.
"Zzzeet-zzzeet!" she calls
to the hummingbird at the window.

While Papa is hurrying off to work,
and Mama is busy with Antonio,
Little Mamá fills two big bowls
with the rice pudding we made yesterday.

"Rice pudding for *breakfast*?" I whisper.
"*Sí, sí,* my little one!" Little Mamá says.
"Pud-*ding.* Eggs, rice, raisins, cinnamon—*delicioso!*"
Even when she forgets about the toast,
my little *mamá* remembers . . .

to pour rivers of cream
on *my* pudding—
just the way I like it.

Sometimes, Little Mamá forgets . . .
how to tie her shoes.
"Two long bunny ears—like this." I show her.
Even though she forgets about loops
and bows and double knots,
my little *mamá* remembers . . .

how to button her favorite dancing shoes.
Little Mamá's satin slippers are yellow now and *so* smooth.
And sometimes when I wear them,

we *twir-r-r-rl* together, my little *mamá* and me.

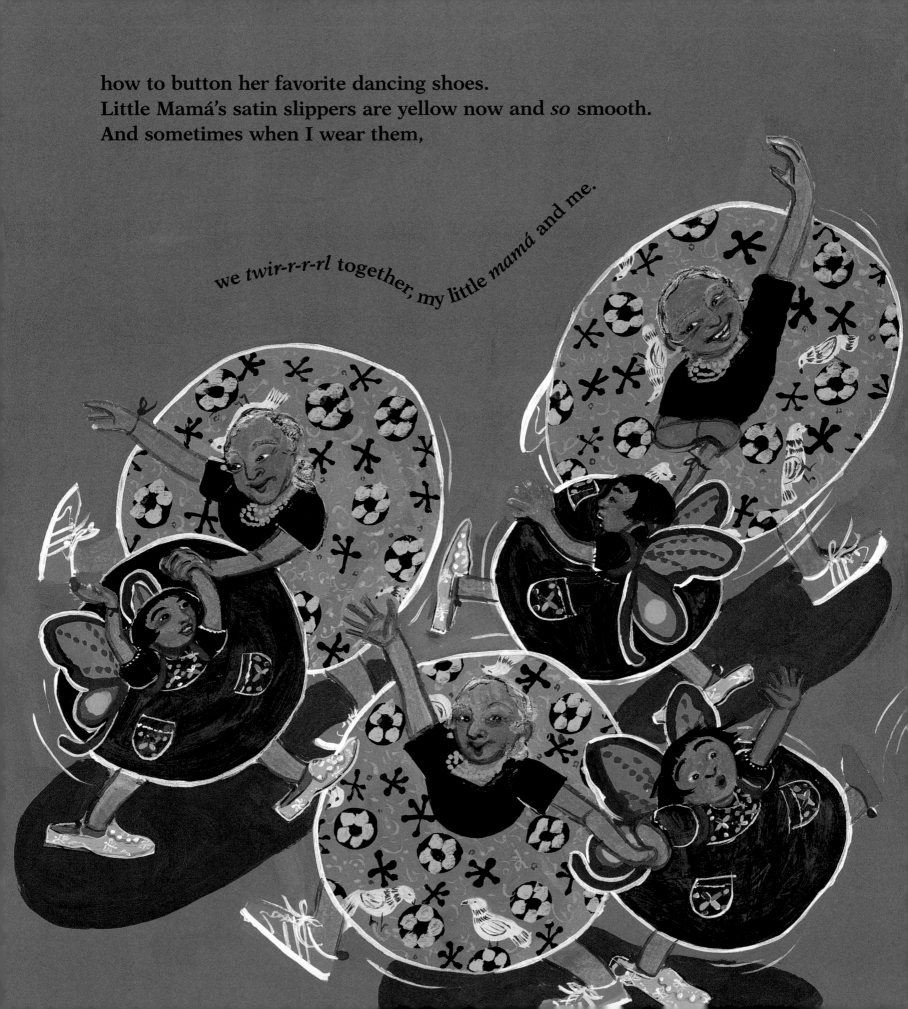

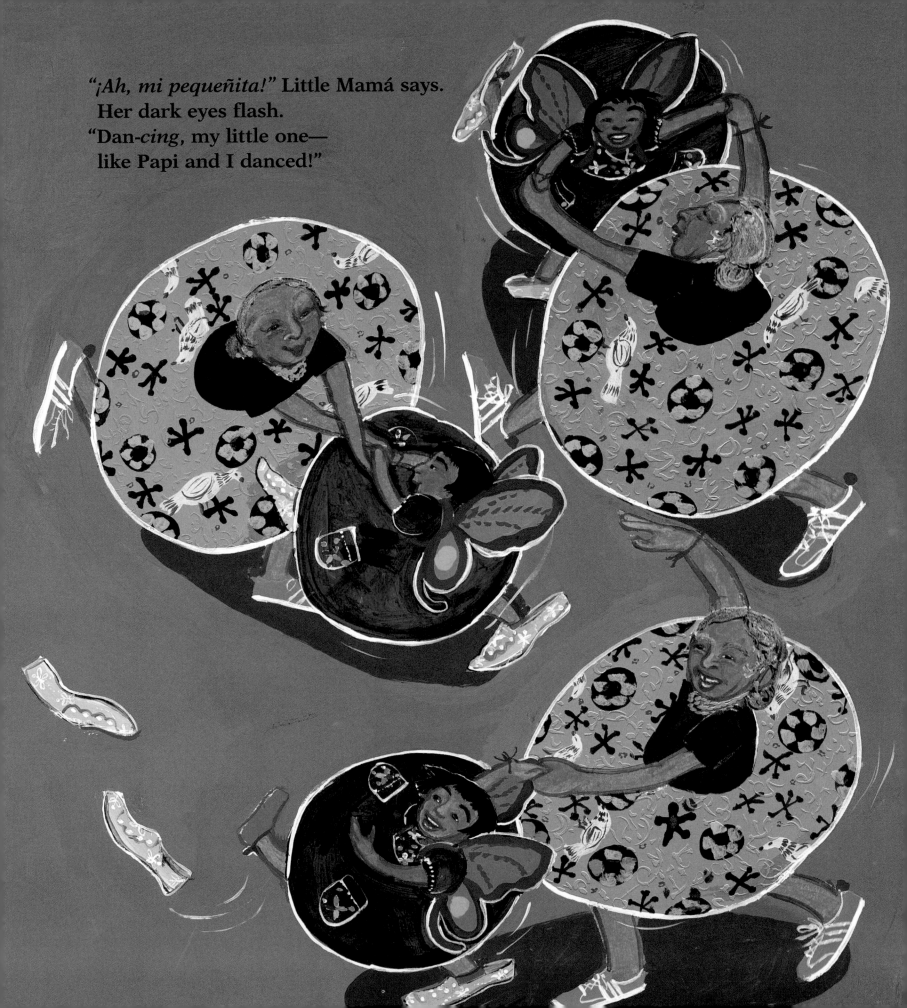

"*¡Ah, mi pequeñita!*" Little Mamá says.
Her dark eyes flash.
"Dan-*cing*, my little one—
like Papi and I danced!"

Some afternoons, when we walk to the park,
my little *mamá* forgets . . .
which way to turn. To the left? To the right?
"*¿A la izquierda? ¿A la derecha?*" she asks.

And sometimes, Little Mamá forgets . . .
to wait for the light to turn green
before she crosses the street.
But even when she forgets that red means STOP!—
my little *mamá* remembers . . .

how to skip, just like I showed her.
And so we do—
Antonio, Mama, Little Mamá, and me.
"*Sí, sí*—all hold hands!" my little *mamá* says.
She laughs and sings
all the way through the park.

When we stop at the marketplace,
my little *mamá* forgets . . .
that Mama says not to sniff and pinch the fruit.
Maybe the oranges and avocados
remind her of the village where
she and her brothers and sisters
picked fruit and played in the sun.

I know all of her stories by heart.
And when Little Mamá talks about that village,
I can almost *see* her
climbing trees and chasing chickens
in sunny Tembabichi.

Little Mamá and Rosa, the baker,
and Francisco, the butcher,
chatter about Mexico like chickadees.
But even when they all seem to forget
that we live in California,
my little *mamá* remembers . . .

to buy chili dogs for Antonio and me.
She gobbles one up, too!

Almost every afternoon,
while Antonio naps and Mama studies,
Little Mamá forgets . . .
that she and Paco and I
are supposed to sleep a little, too.
"I'm too big and too busy to nap!" I say.
"*Sí, sí*—me, too!" says Little Mamá.

She opens her old trunk,
and Paco watches with big green eyes
as shawls and fans and ruffled skirts
swirl in a rainbow around us.

Some evenings, when we make tortillas,
Little Mamá forgets . . .
that there are only five of us for dinner.
I push and pull the mountain of dough
until it's soft and smooth—
just like Little Mamá showed me.

Together, we roll the dough into little balls
that we press as flat as pancakes.
Little Mamá fries the tortillas, and soon—
there are two tall towers of them!
I'm glad my little *mamá* remembers . . .

that my aunt Isabel and uncle Carlos—
and my cousins Clara, Gabe, Carl, and Anna—
like her tortillas, too!
Now there are *twelve* of us for dinner,
counting Paco—
a crowd as big and noisy and happy
as Little Mamá's family must have been,
long ago in Tembabichi.

My cousins spin across the porch
and into the dark.
Our house is quiet again,
buttoned up for the night.

Mama and Papa read to Antonio
while we brush our teeth, Little Mamá and me.
"Up-down, up-down," I remind her,
and we spit into the sink!

Before she tiptoes off to bed,
my little *mamá* remembers . . .
to brush her hair one hundred strokes—
and to brush my hair, too,
until it shines like moonlight.

Almost every day, Little Mamá forgets . . .
names and places and people and words.
She forgets so many things she once knew.
But my pretty grandma, my *bonita abuelita*,
always remembers . . .
to tuck me in with a song and a kiss.

Duérmete mi niña

Luciana María Isabela Gálvez-Molinero.
My little *mamá*'s name is a gentle lullaby.
"*Buenas noches*, my little Luciana!" Little Mamá calls.
"Good night, my little *mamá*. ¡*Te amo!*"